Chapter One

"IOLANTHE."

"What?"

"What are you doing?"

"I'm writing, aren't I? You can see I am. Here's the paper in front of me. This is the pen in my hand."

Jennifer sighed.

"I *know* you're writing, Iolanthe. I just want to know *what* you're writing."

"Why?"

"Because it might give me an idea."

That's the trouble with Jennifer. No ideas. Two legs, two arms, a pretty

1

face – but no imagination. None at all.

"I'm writing a story about a sheep called Hector who's suddenly realized he's going to be eaten."

Jennifer peered over my shoulder, and read aloud.

And so I lay forlornly in my sheep pen, reflecting on the sad fate of all who had lain there before me.

"That's very good."

"Yes," I said. "That's why I want to get on with it."

She sighed again.

"I can't think of anything to write."

She never can.

"I haven't even *started*."

Surprise, surprise.

"You think of something for me."

"Jenni*fer*!"

She shut up for a bit. I carried on, through Hector's desperate dawn escape, his daring capture of the farmer and his wife, the barbecue, and then the visit from the farm inspector.

"And how are Mr and Mrs Crool?"

"Excellent," said Hector. "Very, very tasty. I think the ducklings got the sauce just right."

Now Jennifer was leaning over my arm again.

"Have the animals *eaten* them?"

"Yes. Of course."

She seemed amazed.

"How did you think of *that*?"

"I just did."

"I don't know how you do it," she said crossly. "Miss Hardie says 'Write a story' and I sit here and can't think of a single word to write. You just pick up your pen and out it pours. Sensitive sheep. Cruel farmers. Cannibal cows. And I can't think of *anything*. It's not *fair*."

There must be *something* between Jennifer's ears. She can do maths, and learn poems, and even play the piano.

But every time I hear that old wail of hers ("I can't think of anything to write"), I want to tape her mouth shut. Or fine her fifty pence. Or move, and sit by Sarah. Or complain to Miss Hardie. Or change schools. Or slice off the top of Jennifer's head, and fill her brain up to overflowing with some of my leftover ideas.

I have too many of them. That's my trouble.

Chapter Two

WHEN WE WERE getting ready to go home, I found a rainbow-coloured book on the floor. I picked it up and asked Jennifer, "Did this fall out of your pocket?"

She put her hand out for it.

"Oh, thank you, Iolanthe."

I turned the pretty book over.

"What is it? Is it new?"

"It's a present," she said. "A diary. From my Aunt Muriel. Every single day of the year has a whole glossy blank page to itself, so you can write in it."

"And what have you put in it so far?"

"Nothing much," she admitted.

I opened it at the first page.

Jan 1st. It was quite cold today.

I turned the page. January 2nd was still blank. And so was January 3rd. But on January 4th, she'd spilled out all her secrets.

Mum and I went to the shops.

"So what did you buy," I asked her, "on January 4th?"

She stared at me.

"I can't remember."

"You should have put it in the diary," I said. "That's what it's for."

She snatched it back.

"You know I'm no good at writing."

"That's ideas for Miss Hardie,"

I said. "But this is a diary. You didn't have to make things up. You could have just written down what happened."

"Not much did."

"Then you could have written something else in it," I said. "Like Inner Thoughts."

She looked as blank as January 2nd.

"Inner Thoughts?"

"You know," I said. "Things like Unspoken Fears. Private Worries. Secret Hopes. Everyone has those."

Jennifer gave me a funny look, as if to say, 'Maybe *you* do, Iolanthe. But *I* don't.' Then she went off, to walk home with Sarah. I go the other way. So when I saw the diary on the ground again, just outside school, instead of chasing after the two of them to give it back, I picked it up and took it home with me.

Diaries are deeply private. I know that.

So it sat on the table while I was having tea, and I didn't even touch it.

It sat on the arm of the sofa while I

was watching telly. I didn't even peep inside.

And it sat on the laundry basket while I was having my bath. I didn't even nose through the pages, looking for good bits I'd missed.

I didn't crack until bedtime. Then I read all the bits I'd read before, while Jennifer was watching. (*Jan 1st. It was quite cold today.* Blank. Blank. *Jan 4th. Mum and I went to the shops.*) The next two pages were just two more blanks. Then:

Jan 7th. Nothing much happened.

And that was that.

I'm serious. I turned over every page, and there was no more. Not a single word. And it's the eleventh today.

Sad life.

Chapter Three

I ONLY WROTE in it because it was there. I wasn't being spiteful. It's just that I was tucked up in my bed, not at all tired, with nothing else to do. My pen was practically *waving* at me out of my school bag. And the next page in the diary was so smooth and white and empty, it seemed to be *begging* for help.

"Help! Help!"
The words still ring in my ears.
"Help! Help!"
Today (January 11th) *I saved a little*

boy's life. I'm
not that brave. In fact
Iolanthe, who sits next
to me in class, often
says I'm a wimp. But
when I saw that poor child
drowning in the river on the way to school, I
didn't stop to think. I just tore off my clothes,
and jumped, in my knickers, into the freezing
water.

The boy was panicking.

"Stop struggling," I warned. "Or I'll have to
knock you out."

He kept on thrashing, so I bopped him, hard. His eyes rolled horribly, but he was no more trouble. So slowly, slowly I hauled him back to the bank, and dragged him out.

A woman flew out of the bushes.

"My son!" she cried. "My own dear son! How cold and wet you are!"

She scooped him up, and ran off towards a

little house some way along the river.

I wondered whether to go after her. But then the school bell rang.

Five to nine!

Quickly, I pulled on my clothes and ran. My knickers are still wet. But otherwise I'm fine. Just happy to have saved a life. And happy I wasn't late.

Good story, I thought. And it just fitted neatly on the page. So how was I to know it was going to cause so much trouble? How was I to know Miss Hardic would look round the classroom the very next morning, and then pick on Jennifer?

"Remember those stories I asked you all to write yesterday? Jennifer, why don't you read us yours?"

Jennifer looked anxious.

"I didn't really get started," she admitted.

Miss Hardie looked so cross that I thought I'd better come to Jennifer's rescue.

"She was too busy writing in her diary," I explained.

"Right, then," Miss Hardie said cheerfully. "Why don't you read us some of that instead?"

Jennifer picked it up, and flicked through the first few pages.

"There isn't really much in it."

Miss Hardie was getting cross again now.

"Well, read it anyway," she snapped.

So Jennifer began to read.

"Jan 1st. It was quite cold today. Jan 4th. Mum and I went to the shops."

Her voice trailed off. She turned the next few pages rather hopelessly, waiting for Miss Hardie's explosion.

And then, suddenly, like manna from heaven, she came across my bit.

"Help! Help!"
The words still ring in my ears.

I thought she read the story out rather well, considering it came as such a surprise. I couldn't understand

why she got so ratty after. Everyone was crowding round her, telling her how *brave* she was, and how *exciting* it must have been, and how *rude* the boy's mother was not to come back and say thank you to the person who had just saved her poor son from a watery grave.

And all Jennifer could do was hiss at me tearfully:

"How *could* you, Iolanthe! Wet knickers! I've never had wet knickers in my life!"

Chapter Four

WE MADE UP later that morning. We had to, because Miss Hardie got so fed up with the noise, she made everybody in the class settle down and write a story called *Time Travel*.

Jennifer was stuck, and I needed to borrow her second-best ballpoint.

"I'll only lend it to you if you share your idea with me."

"I'll only share my idea with you if you stop being mad at me."

"All right."

"All right."

So I shared my idea with her. It was brilliant.

"Pretend we have to come back to school in fifty years' time, for Open Day. Just write down what you think this place will be like by the time you and I are about sixty."

She stared at me admiringly.

"You're so *clever*, Iolanthe."

"Yes, I am," I said. But she didn't look shocked, like she usually does

when I say that, because she'd already
started. I read it over her shoulder. It
was really dull. All about how much
taller the trees had grown, and how
the entrance hall was painted blue
now, not green. And how all the pupils
had tiny computers built into their
desks, and the teachers took them on
rocket trips to the moon instead of
bus rides to the museum.

"Stop reading over my shoulder,"

she complained. "Get on with your own work."

So I did.

It hardly seems over half a century since I was last here, I wrote. *Personally, I still feel, and look, like the vibrant and beautiful young girl I was then. But the rust on the old school gates is something shocking. And, golly, there's been some litter dropped in sixty years. I had to wade through lolly wrappers to reach the front door.*

And what a shock greeted me there!

Miss Hardie (far too old to teach, poor dear) almost fell off her zimmer frame trying to open the door to me. Her hair was snowy-white. The veins on her hands looked like tree roots. Her ill-fitting false teeth clacked horribly as she spoke.

"Who is it?"

She peered at me blindly. Then:

"Is it –? Can it be – ? Yes!" she cried in her

cracked and quavering old voice. "It's Iolanthe Jones! Come in, my dear! How lovely to see you! You were always my favourite pupil."

I smiled my usual modest smile as Miss Hardie's lined face suddenly became even more wrinkled.

"Now, who was that little girl who used to sit next to you, Iolanthe? That poor, pathetic creature who could never think of any –

Sensing danger, I looked up. Jennifer was watching me very closely indeed.

– *names for her pet kittens*, I wrote hastily.

I thought I'd be safe with that. (Jennifer's allergic to fur.) But, no. She went straight into a giant sulk.

"You're *horrible*, Iolanthe," she said. "You're so mean that I'm phoning my mum to tell her not to bother to come and pick me up at lunchtime. Because I won't need to go shopping for a new

frock, because I'm not coming to your
party."

"You can't phone her. The phone's
broken. And I wasn't being mean.
I wasn't writing about you. I was
writing about a person I haven't even
sat by yet. That's what Time Travel's
all about."

I don't know if she believed me. I
know she didn't try to phone. But,

then again, I didn't really expect her to, because if there's one thing that Jennifer absolutely loves, it's a party. Even one of mine.

Chapter Five

IT WAS HER own fault for getting back so late. If she'd been here, I'd have been able to do the same as everyone else, and work in a pair. But since I was a leftover, Miss Hardie said firmly, "Do something useful while you're waiting, Iolanthe."

So I wrote in the diary. I wrote in the diary because no one else was using it. All Jennifer had written was:
Jan 13th. The sky's a bit pink today.

I started on January 14th.

"No! Not pink! Never pink!"

"Please, Mother," I begged. "Oh, let me buy a pink frock to go to Iolanthe's party."

My mother shrieked in horror.

"No! Never pink! Not after what happened to your Great Aunt Lucy."

"What happened to Great Aunt Lucy?"

"It's too terrible to tell."

I begged. I pleaded. I even wept. And, finally, my mother told me.

"Your Great Aunt Lucy knew that we had a ghost. Dozens of people had seen The Child In Pink. She floated in and out of walls, and groaned at midnight, and on the stormiest nights her sobs were heard in the nursery. Everyone knew her story. She was a disobedient child. Her mother had told her a hundred times: 'Stay away from the nasty dark cellars.' But would she listen? No! She wandered in and out, and one day, she got lost and disappeared."

"What did they do?"

"They searched, of course. High and low,

calling her name. But by the time they found
her, she was dead. Quite dead!"

"Quite dead?"

"Well, not quite dead, because from that
day on, she haunted them. In and out of
walls. Groaning and sobbing. Until the day
your Great Aunt Lucy wore pink to go to a
party. Lucy put on her frock, and then, with
half an hour to spare, she wandered off,
down to the cellars."

"No!"

"Yes! And just like The Child In Pink, she wandered in and out of cold dark places. Some say she saw a child her own age, beckoning. And others say she heard a sweet little voice. "Don't go to that party. Come to mine!" All that we know is that your Great Aunt Lucy was never seen alive again. And now, on stormy nights, instead of sobbing, we hear peals of laughter. At midnight, instead of *groans, we hear two sweet voices singing. And instead of seeing one child in pink float through the walls, people see two, hand in hand. And people say —*

Jennifer came rushing back in then, all red-faced, holding a great big carrier bag.

"You're terribly late," Miss Hardie scolded her. "The bell rang a long time ago."

"Mum says she's sorry and it will never happen again," Jennifer panted. "It's just that I had to get a frock for Iolanthe's party. The traffic both ways was frightful. And it took us forever to find something the right colour."

She fell in her seat, still panting.

"Which colour's that, then?" I asked.

"Pink," Jennifer said proudly.

Just as proudly, I pointed to the first line of my story.

"No! Not pink! Never pink!"

Jennifer snatched her diary and read through what I'd written. She was so cross again, she wouldn't speak to me the whole afternoon. And I think she

only came to my party because her
mother made her.

She wore blue.

Chapter Six

I WANTED THE diary so much.

"Please!" I begged Jennifer. "It's
wasted on someone like you. You
hardly use it. *Please* give it to me."

"What will you give me for it?"

I lifted up my desk lid.

"Nothing," I said sadly. "There's
nothing in here anyone would want."

Jennifer shrugged.

"I'll just keep it for now, then."

"But you don't write anything in it!"

"That's because nothing happens."

"No, it's not."

She let me fill in the empty pages,

though. The back ones she hadn't used. So on the January 2nd page, I wrote a horror story about a trumpet that could call freshly dead people out of their graves.

On the January 3rd page, I made a list of all my Unspoken Fears, in code. (Mind your own business.)

Two pages later, I wrote a poem called *Stamping on Granny's Daisies*.

She wanted it back then, so I let her have it. But she couldn't think of anything to write.

On the January 6th page, I put down my Private Worries in strict alphabetical order. (Mind your own business again.)

On the blank page of January 8th, I started on a list of Secret Hopes. But there was only one. (That Jennifer would give me the diary.) So I gave up, and started another ghost tale.

And it was as well I hadn't used up the space, because the story got so complicated, it went on through blank pages January 9th and 10th. And even then I had to finish it in tiny writing, so as not to get tangled in *"Help! Help!"* on the 11th.

On the January 12th page, I wrote a letter begging for the diary.

Dear, sweet and lovely Jennifer,
All of my life, I have longed for a diary like this one to write all my ideas and thoughts in. It's kind of you to lend it when I ask. But borrowing's not like having. This diary and I were made for one another. We shouldn't be parted for a single hour.

And I kept on, for the whole page, with Jennifer pretending she wasn't reading it over my shoulder.

"What now?" I asked her. "I've run out of room until tomorrow."

"Maybe I'll use up tomorrow's page myself."

"I doubt it."

"I *might*," she snapped.

I didn't want to argue. (I was still hoping she would give it to me.) So I went back and filled in all her old half-used days.

I stared at her January 1st (*It was quite cold today.*) and then picked up my pen.

But not cold enough to stop noble and kind Iolanthe taking soup to the poor. From my window, I watched her pick her way over snow and ice to old Mrs Morris's hovel. Inside that rude hut lie sixteen shivering children, all half-starved. If it weren't for dear Iolanthe —

Miss Hardie interrupted me in mid-flow.

"Iolanthe! Come up to my desk, please. I want a little word with you."

You couldn't really call what she had with me 'a little word'. It was more like a giant great lecture, all

about 'pushing my luck', and 'going
too far', and 'the point at which
imagination shades into simple
rudeness'.

I had to say sorry about a million times, and then stick clean white paper over most of my Time Travel story and write in something else over the top. It took a lot of time, so it wasn't till the next day that I got round to filling in Jennifer's mostly-empty January 4th (*Mum and I went to the shops.*)

Mum and I went to the shops.

"Quick!" she said. "Stuff this up your pinny, Jennifer, and I'll hide this in my bag."

"Mother!" I said. "You mustn't shoplift! It's quite wrong!"

Her face cracked into an evil scowl.

"I'm not your mother!" she cried. "It's time you knew, Jennifer. There was a mix-up at the hospital when you were born. This high-born lady and myself were sharing a room. The cots lay side by side. And in the middle of the night —

I broke off. I had to. Jennifer was stabbing me with her pen.

"Stop it!" she ordered. "Stop it!"

Normally, I'd have argued. But I'd been in such trouble already that week that I just shrugged, and moved on to her January 7th. *(Nothing much happened today.)*

Nothing much happened today. After the spaceship landed and all the blobmen had blobbled down the ladder into the woods –

"Iolanthe!"

"Yes, Miss Hardie?"

"That's not your workbook you're writing in, is it?"

"No, Miss Hardie. It's Jennifer's diary."

"Give it back."

Does *no one* want me to be happy?

No one at *all*? I sulked for the rest of
the day. I tried to tell myself that
pretty rainbow-coloured books don't
matter. It's the stories that count. But
I wanted Jennifer's diary *so much*. If I
could get her to give it to me, for
keeps, I could start off from January
15th. That would mean three hundred
and fifty pages left.

All blank and gleaming and glossy.
And all mine.

What I needed was something to trade. But I had nothing Jennifer might want. My desk was full of rubbish. Most of the stuff I have at home has to be shared with my sister. And I owe pocket money for a hundred years.

But "Curly hair, curly thoughts" says my granny.

Let's hope she's right . . .

Chapter Seven

THE VERY NEXT morning, I opened Jennifer's diary to January 15th.

"Don't you start writing on today's page," she told me. "I might want to use it myself later."

See how this sharing isn't working out?

I flicked back to the last only slightly-used page.

Jan 13th. The sky's a bit pink today.

I gazed at it, chewing my pen and screwing up my face. I drummed my fingers on the desk. I rolled my eyes.

"What's the matter?" asked Jennifer.

"I can't think of anything to write," I told her.

Jennifer stared.

"What? *You?*"

"Yes," I said snappily. "*Me.*"

Jennifer looked anxious.

"Are you ill, Iolanthe?"

"No. I'm not ill."

"Then what's happened?"

"Nothing's happened," I told her. "It's just that I don't seem to have any ideas."

"That's strange, for you."

"Yes, isn't it?"

We stared at it together for a while.

The sky's a bit pink today.

Then Jennifer said guiltily, "Maybe it's my fault. I was the one who wrote it, after all. And it is a bit boring."

Bit boring? *The sky's a bit pink today* is START ME OFF WITH A YAWN. But I was too canny to say so.

"Not at all. And, anyhow, I ought to be able to think of *something.*"

We both stared some more. I felt it was important to keep her attention, so:

"Suppose . . .?" I said hesitantly.

Then, shaking my head, "No. Forget it."

That set her off.

"What about . . .?" As usual, she stopped. "No. That's no good."

It's not my style, but I was getting in the swing of it.

"What if . . .?" I broke off. "No.

That's stupid."

Encouraged, she tried again herself.

"Could you . . .?" Sadly, she brushed the idea aside. "No. That's hopeless, too."

I turned to look at her with wide, sincere eyes.

"Jennifer," I said. "I want to tell you I'm sorry. I've been a brute. A horrid, impatient brute. I never thought about how awful it must feel to be a person who has no ideas. I promise I'll never again tease you, or get crabby when you can't think of anything to write."

Her eyes lit up.

"Really?"

"Really," I said. "In fact, I *almost* feel that if I ever had two ideas in future, and you had none, I'd give you one of mine."

She turned to look at me closely.

"You almost think that?"

"Yes, *almost.*"

She picked up the diary and gazed at it thoughtfully.

"Do you think having this might just push you over?"

"Push me over?"

"From *almost* to *definitely*."

"Yes, it might." I laid a finger on it and shut my eyes. "In fact, I have a feeling it might even help me get my ideas back."

She shoved it into my hand.

"Here. Take it. It's yours."

"Really? For keeps?"

"For keeps."

I held it tightly, and stared into space.

"I think it's working," I said hopefully. "Yes. Yes! I believe it's working. In fact, at this very moment, I feel an idea welling up."

"*Two*," Jennifer said firmly.

"Yes. *Two* ideas," I agreed hastily. "One for me, one for you."

"That's better," she said tartly.

I'm keeping hers, of course, until she needs it. I've started off on mine.

The sky's a bit pink today. Ever since Venus exploded, and shattered Mars, the colours have been startling. The few of us who weren't blinded by the flashes sit by the fire –

And it's a good idea. But pretending I'd run out of ideas was even better.

I can't write that one in the diary, though.

Jennifer might see.